I Wonder Why

Vultures Are Bald

and Other Questions About Birds

Amanda O'Neill

Kingfisher

KINGFISHER
An imprint of Larousse plc
Elsley House, 24–30 Great Titchfield Street
London W1P 7AD

First published by Kingfisher 1997
(hb) 10 9 8 7 6 5 4 3 2 1
(pb) 10 9 8 7 6 5 4 3 2 1
Copyright © Larousse plc 1997

A CIP catalogue record for this book is
available from the British Library

ISBN   0 7534 0162 2 (hb)
       0 7534 0191 6 (pb)

Series editor: Clare Oliver
Series designer: David West Children's Books
Author: Amanda O'Neill
Consultant: Michael Chinery
Editor: Claire Llewellyn
Art editor: Christina Fraser
Picture researcher: Amanda Francis
Illustrations: Andrew Beckett (Garden Studio) 22–23; Chris Forsey
   10–11; Ian Jackson 4–5, 8–9, 16–17, 26–27, 30–31; Tony
   Kenyon (BL Kearley) all cartoons; Martin Knowleden (Virgil
   Pomfret) 14–15; Terence Lambert cover, 12–13, 18–19,
   24–25; Dan Wright 6–7, 28–29; David Wright (Kathy
   Jakeman) 20–21.

CONTENTS

Which bird is a giant?

The ostrich is the biggest living bird. From top to toe it's over 2.5 metres tall – that's about as high as the ceiling! And it's heavy, too, weighing about the same as a Shetland pony!

● The biggest flying bird is the wandering albatross. From wingtip to wingtip it's as long as a family car!

● The ostrich can't fly. But it can run from danger at up to 72 kilometres per hour – that's faster than a racehorse.

Ostrich

Which bird flies fastest?

Eider duck

The eider duck can fly along at up to 100 kilometres per hour. But the real record-breaker is the peregrine falcon. It swoops down on its prey at over 200 kilometres per hour, making it the fastest animal on Earth.

● The fastest swimmer is the gentoo penguin. It can race through the water at up to 27 kilometres per hour – that's three times faster than the fastest person.

Peregrine falcon

Which is the smallest bird?

● The African kori bustard is the heaviest flying bird. Sometimes it even has trouble getting off the ground!

In tropical rainforests, many of the birds are smaller than the butterflies. The Cuban bee hummingbird is probably the smallest of all. It's about as big as the eye of an ostrich – and can perch on the end of a pencil.

5

Why are birds special?

Birds are not the only animals with wings, the only ones that lay eggs, or the only ones with beaks. But they are the only creatures in the whole wide world that have feathers.

● Birds aren't the only animals to fly. Bats do, too – and they're mammals.

● Birds aren't the only animals to have a beak. The duck-billed platypus does, too.

● Birds aren't the only animals to lay eggs. Tortoises and other reptiles do, too.

● All birds have wings, but not all of them can fly. Some creep, hop, or run along the ground; others swim like seals in the sea.

● There are 30 birds in the world for every man, woman and child.

Which birds have scales?

All of them! Birds' feet and legs are covered with scaly skin, just like the skin of snakes and lizards. That's why you never see birds wearing shoes and socks! But the scales don't stop there. A bird's feathers may seem soft to the touch, but they're made of tough, horny stuff – just like scales.

Why do birds fly?

Flying is a great way to escape from enemies. With a few flaps of its wings, a bird can get to a safe perch well out of the reach of a hungry cat! Being able to fly also helps birds to move quickly from one feeding ground to another, and to catch insects that buzz through the air.

● The handsome roller bird is a true acrobat. When chasing insects, it performs somersaults in the air.

How do birds fly?

The usual way for a bird to fly is to flap its wings up and down. This pushes it through the air, just as oars push a boat through the water. But it's hard work, so some birds save energy by gliding. Once they've built up speed, they spread out their wings, and let breezy air currents carry them along.

● Like planes, birds need to be strong but light. To keep their weight down, they have hollow or paper-thin bones.

● Hummingbirds are the only birds that can fly backwards. They can also fly forwards, sideways and upside-down!

● The common swift spends nearly its whole life in the air. It even sleeps on the wing!

z z z z z z z

z z z z

How many feathers does a bird have?

The bigger a bird is, the more feathers it has. A hummingbird has about 900 feathers, while a swan has 25,000! Feathers come in all different shapes and sizes. Soft downy feathers keep the bird warm, others keep it waterproof in the rain, and the strongest feathers give it the power to fly.

● Birds have long tail feathers, smooth wing and body feathers, and fluffy down feathers. Down is warmer than fur – it's like a bird's woolly underwear.

Tail feathers

Golden pheasant

Pheasant

Body feathers

Parrot

Goose

African grey parrot

Scarlet macaw

Down feather

Guinea fowl

10

● Every wing feather is made up of hundreds of hair-like strands. These zip together with tiny hooks to make a smooth, strong blade.

Why are vultures bald?

Vultures are messy eaters. They feed on dead animals, pushing their heads right inside the bodies to tear into the meat. If they had head feathers, they'd get dirty and sticky, and would be almost impossible to clean. That's why vultures are much better off being bald.

● Feathers work so hard that they wear out. The bird grows a new set each year and the old ones gradually fall out. This is called moulting.

Turkey

Flamingo

Wing feathers

Macaw

Seagull

Parrot

● Before pens were invented, people wrote with quills. These were large feathers, sharpened at the end and dipped in ink.

Who eats with giant tweezers?

A hungry toucan pushes leaves apart with its big, long beak. Then the bird uses the tip of its beak very delicately, like tweezers, to pick fruit off the branch. Next it tosses the fruit up in the air and snaps it up as it falls.

● The Galápagos woodpecker finch is the only bird to use a fork! It grasps a twig in its beak to poke out insects from holes in the trees.

...a pair of pliers?

Crossbills feed on the seeds inside pine cones, and they have a very special beak to prise them out. The top half of the beak twists over the bottom half. This helps the birds to get a good grip and force the cones open.

● The sword-billed hummingbird's beak is longer than its body. It's like a straw to suck nectar from deep inside a flower.

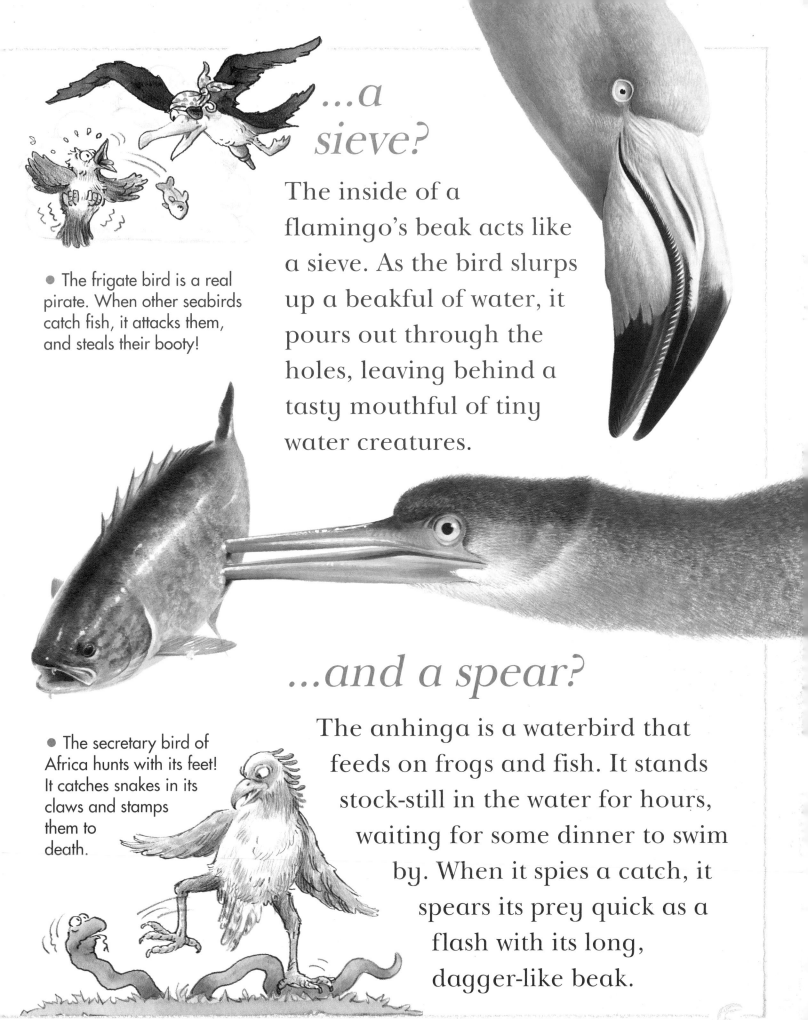

...a sieve?

The inside of a flamingo's beak acts like a sieve. As the bird slurps up a beakful of water, it pours out through the holes, leaving behind a tasty mouthful of tiny water creatures.

● The frigate bird is a real pirate. When other seabirds catch fish, it attacks them, and steals their booty!

...and a spear?

The anhinga is a waterbird that feeds on frogs and fish. It stands stock-still in the water for hours, waiting for some dinner to swim by. When it spies a catch, it spears its prey quick as a flash with its long, dagger-like beak.

● The secretary bird of Africa hunts with its feet! It catches snakes in its claws and stamps them to death.

Which is the biggest eagle?

The harpy eagle is bigger than a Great Dane, and is the largest and most powerful of the eagles. It lives in the rainforests of South America, where it chases monkeys through the trees, grabbing them with its deadly claws!

● An eagle's feet are deadly weapons. Its toes are strong enough to crush its prey, and its claws are razor-sharp.

● Birds are some of the best fishermen in the world. When an osprey dives into the water, it can catch fish more than half its own size.

● Vultures sometimes eat so much that they can't take off after their meal.

Which birds have sneaky wings?

Most owls hunt at night, swooping down silently on rabbits, mice and other tasty prey. The hunters have special fringed wing feathers, which can beat the air without making a sound. That way, their prey doesn't hear them coming, and has no time to escape!

● The Everglade kite lives on water snails. Its hooked beak is just the right shape to winkle a snail from its shell.

● Owls eat their prey whole. Later, they cough up all the bones and fur in a neat little sausage-shaped pellet.

Why does a budgie cock its head?

A budgie's eyes are on the side of its head so that it can see all around. But seeing things close up is harder work. The bird has to cock its head and aim a special viewer in the middle of its eye – a bit like when you aim your camera to take a photo.

● The woodcock has the most extraordinary eyes. Without moving its head, it can see what's going on in front, behind and even above.

Which bird steers with its ears?

The South American oilbird makes its nest deep in a cave. It can't see in the darkness so, as it flies, the oilbird makes non-stop clicking noises, which echo when they bounce off the cave walls. By listening to where the echoes come from, the oilbird knows exactly where the cave walls are.

● Ducks have a pair of see-through eyelids that protect their eyes when they dive. The eyelids are just like swimming goggles, helping ducks to see under water.

Which bird sniffs all night?

The New Zealand kiwi hunts at night, using its nose to sniff out worms, insects and other tasty titbits. Unlike other birds' nostrils, a kiwi's are at the end of its long beak. To find itself some dinner, all it has to do is stick its beak in the soil and take a jolly good sniff!

● The honeyguide feeds on beeswax. When it's sniffed out a bees' nest, it sometimes leads people to the spot and waits for them to break the nest open. Then the people can eat the honey and the honeyguide gets the wax.

Who's the best-dressed bird?

Male birds of paradise grow beautiful lacy feathers during the breeding season. When a female comes by, all the males hang upside-down to show off their stunning plumage. It's a beauty contest, and the female picks the bird with the finest feathers to be her mate!

Do all birds sing?

Just over half of all birds sing, but the rest are far from silent. Geese honk, owls hoot, gulls mew, and the Australian kookaburra seems to laugh. It's mostly male birds that sing – either to attract a mate or to warn other males to clear off their patch.

● In some New York houses, parrots are trained as burglar alarms! They let out a piercing shriek if someone breaks in.

● The male palm cockatoo attracts a mate by playing her a tune. He grasps a twig in one foot and uses it as a drumstick to beat a hollow log.

Which bird looks a fright?

If you scare a hawk-eagle, it'll probably scare you back! This bird has a crest of long feathers on its head. When it feels in danger, these feathers stand on end. This makes the eagle look look bigger and fiercer than it really is – with any luck, it will frighten away the enemy.

Which is the cleverest builder?

The male weaver bird has to prove he's a good nest-builder before he can win a mate. He hangs from a branch, weaving long strips of grass into a hollow ball. If his nest is good enough, the female will line it with feathers. If not, he has to start all over again!

● Many birds spend the night huddled together in sheltered spots. It helps them to keep warm, especially in winter. This is called roosting.

Which nest has central heating?

The Australian mallee fowl lays her eggs inside a big pile of leaves. As they rot, the leaves give off heat and keep the eggs nice and warm. Every day the father checks the nest with his beak. If it's too hot, he makes a hole to cool it down.

● Mockingbirds on the Galápagos Islands snatch hair from people's heads to line their nests.

Who lives in a city by the sea?

For many seabirds, a cliff is the perfect place to nest – it's out of reach for hunters and handy for fishing. Thousands of birds lay their eggs on the narrow ledges or nest in cracks in the rocks. With all those birds fighting for space, it's like a kind of city – crowded, smelly and very noisy!

When do birds have teeth?

Inside the egg, a baby chick grows a little tooth on its beak. When the chick is ready to hatch, it uses this tooth to chip away at the eggshell from the inside. The baby bird never needs its tooth again, so it drops off soon after hatching.

• A kingfisher's nest is a stinking mess of fish bones and droppings. As soon as they leave the nest, the chicks dive in the river for a good wash!

1 A baby bird chips a hole in the shell.

2 More holes make a dotted line.

Which eggs look like pebbles?

If you're walking on a pebbly beach in the spring, watch where you're putting your feet! Some of those round, speckly pebbles may be a plover's eggs. Plovers make their nests on open ground, but their eggs are perfectly hidden – because they look just like pebbles.

• Baby birds are hungry little things. A mother wren may feed her young hundreds of times a day!

• Flamingo chicks feed on a runny food made by their parents. It's rather like mammals' milk – except that it's red not white!

Who starts life with a jump?

Mallard ducks often nest in holes in the trees, so their ducklings hatch high off the ground. How do they get down? Easy! When their mother calls, they jump out and tumble to the ground. They're so light that they don't need a parachute, and they all land safe and sound.

3 The end of the shell breaks away…

4 …and a damp duckling wriggles out.

5 Now the baby bird is ready to explore.

• A duck egg hatches about four weeks after it has been laid. Hatching can take anything from an hour or two to a whole day!

Why do geese take a winter holiday?

Brent geese fly from one land to another when the seasons change. This is called migration. The birds spend summer in the far north, raising their chicks on grasses and other plants. But if they stayed on in winter, they'd starve! So each autumn they fly to warmer lands.

● It gets so cold in Antarctica that some penguins migrate northwards to South America. They don't fly, of course – they swim!

How do they know when to go?

In autumn, the days grow cooler and shorter. This is a signal to migrating birds that it will soon be time to leave. They eat extra food, fattening themselves up for the journey ahead. Then on a fine day they gather together and fly away.

● The tiny rufous hummingbird spends summer in Alaska and winter in Mexico. That's a round trip of at least 9,600 kilometres!

How do they find their way?

Scientists aren't sure how migrating birds find their way. Some birds seem to know which way to go, as if they had a compass inside them. Others may steer by the sun, moon and stars. And older birds probably remember landmarks, such as rivers and hills.

● Flying long distances uses up lots of energy. Weary birds stop off on the way to rest and fill up with food.

25

Which bird goes to sea?

The great wandering albatross spends most of its life at sea. This huge bird glides for hours on the wild ocean winds. Sometimes sailors see it following their ships across the southern seas.

Which birds walk on water?

When they're fishing in the sea, tiny storm petrels look as though they are walking on the water. They're not – they are actually fluttering above the surface, dipping their feet in the waves. Then they paddle like mad to keep themselves steady in the wind.

Which bird wears a crash helmet?

Gannets are wonderful divers. They dive into the sea from a great height to catch their fishy dinner. But smacking into the water could give them a headache. That's why they have a thick bony skull like a crash helmet, to protect them when they hit the water.

Who likes to paddle in the mud?

Wading birds love the sticky mud at the mouth of a river. Huge flocks of them paddle about in it for hours, sticking in their beaks to hunt out worms, crabs and crunchy shellfish.

● A puffin can carry home as many as 40 fish in its mouth. Little ridges along the beak give it an extra-firm grip.

How do penguins stand the cold?

● Penguin chicks snuggle between their parent's feet to keep warm.

The emperor penguin is the only animal to survive the Antarctic winter on land. Penguins have a thick coat of feathers, and an even thicker coat of fat under their skin. Even with their double overcoats, the birds huddle in huge crowds to keep warm in the biting winds.

● The snowy owl is a hardy bird. To keep out the Arctic chill, it has extra-thick feathers on its legs and feet – just like a warm pair of leggings.

● The ptarmigan lives in the far north. During the summer, its feathers are brown. But every autumn, it grows a new coat of white feathers – an excellent disguise to fool hunters in the snow.

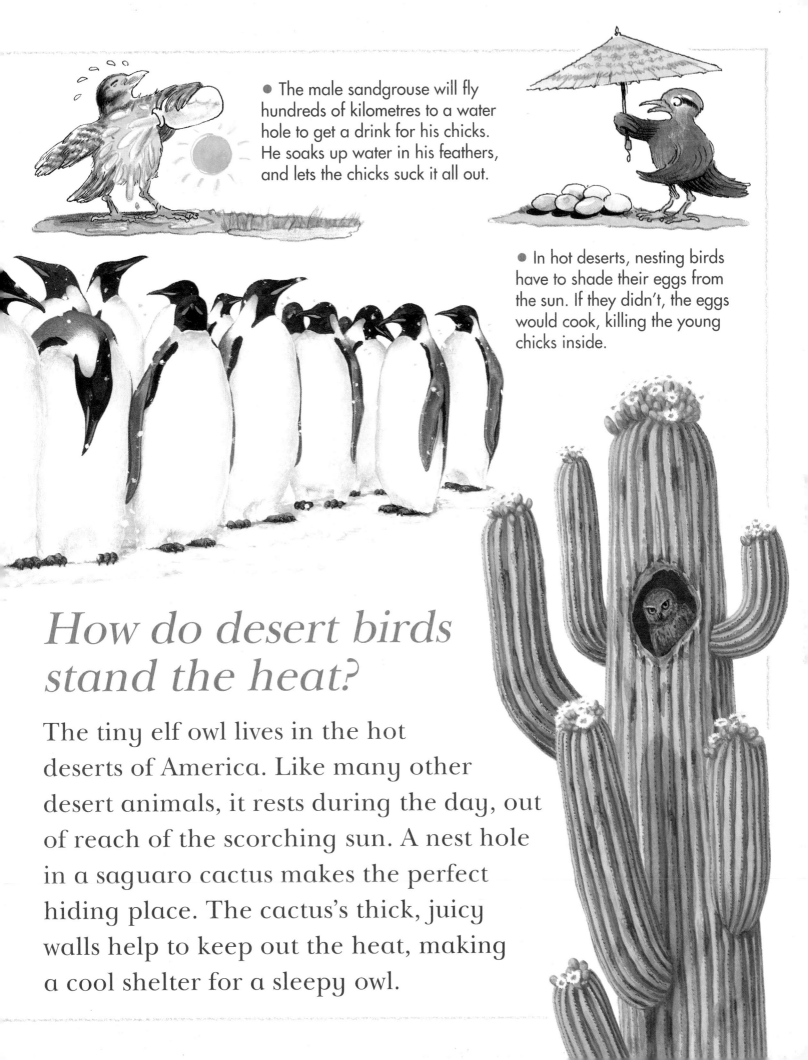

● The male sandgrouse will fly hundreds of kilometres to a water hole to get a drink for his chicks. He soaks up water in his feathers, and lets the chicks suck it all out.

● In hot deserts, nesting birds have to shade their eggs from the sun. If they didn't, the eggs would cook, killing the young chicks inside.

How do desert birds stand the heat?

The tiny elf owl lives in the hot deserts of America. Like many other desert animals, it rests during the day, out of reach of the scorching sun. A nest hole in a saguaro cactus makes the perfect hiding place. The cactus's thick, juicy walls help to keep out the heat, making a cool shelter for a sleepy owl.

Why do people build nests for birds?

Some birds of prey are rare today because people once hunted them or destroyed their homes. So bird lovers are helping these birds to make a comeback by building nesting platforms in out-of-the-way places. As soon as the birds move in, people guard the nests so that the chicks can grow up in peace.

● Ospreys are fishing hawks that once nested in England, but not any more. To encourage them to return, young birds are being moved from their nests in Scotland to new homes by an English lake.

● Every country has special groups of people who try to protect birds. Why not think about joining one?